Communities Then and Now

Katie Peters

GRL Consultants,
Diane Craig and Monica Marx,
Certified Literacy Specialists

Lerner Publications ◆ Minneapolis

Note from a GRL Consultant
This Pull Ahead leveled book has been carefully designed for beginning readers. A team of guided reading literacy experts has reviewed and leveled the book to ensure readers pull ahead and experience success.

Copyright © 2021 by Lerner Publishing Group, Inc.

All rights reserved. International copyright secured. No part of this book may be reproduced, stored in a retrieval system, or transmitted in any form or by any means—electronic, mechanical, photocopying, recording, or otherwise—without the prior written permission of Lerner Publishing Group, Inc., except for the inclusion of brief quotations in an acknowledged review.

Lerner Publications Company
An imprint of Lerner Publishing Group, Inc.
241 First Avenue North
Minneapolis, MN 55401 USA

For reading levels and more information, look up this title at www.lernerbooks.com.

Main body text set in Memphis Pro 24/39
Typeface provided by Linotype.

Photo Acknowledgments
The images in this book are used with the permission of: © anilakkus/iStockphoto, p. 3; © jmsilva/iStockphoto, pp. 8, 9, 16 (airport); © Jonny Essex/iStockphoto, pp. 10, 11; © kelvinjay/iStockphoto, pp. 6, 7, 16 (homes); © Kirkikis/iStockphoto, pp. 14, 15, 16 (park); © MasaoTaira/iStockphoto, pp. 12, 13, 16 (mall); © WendellandCarolyn/iStockphoto, pp. 4, 5.

Front cover: © zimmytws/Shutterstock

Library of Congress Cataloging-in-Publication Data

Names: Peters, Katie, author.
Title: Communities then and now / Katie Peters.
Description: Minneapolis : Lerner Publications, 2020. | Series: My community | Includes index. | Audience: Ages 4–7 | Audience: Grades K–1 | Summary: "This nonfiction title features carefully leveled text and engages emergent readers with its vivid photographs of a changing neighborhood. Pairs with the fiction title Grandpa's Photos"— Provided by publisher.
Identifiers: LCCN 2019046317 (print) | LCCN 2019046318 (ebook) | ISBN 9781541590151 (library binding) | ISBN 9781728403014 (paperback) | ISBN 9781728400570 (ebook)
Subjects: LCSH: Communities—Juvenile literature.
Classification: LCC HM756 .P48 2020 (print) | LCC HM756 (ebook) | DDC 307—dc23

LC record available at https://lccn.loc.gov/2019046317
LC ebook record available at https://lccn.loc.gov/2019046318

Manufactured in the United States of America
4-52779-48069-3/2/2022

Contents

Communities Then
  and Now.............4

Did You See It?........16

Index...................16

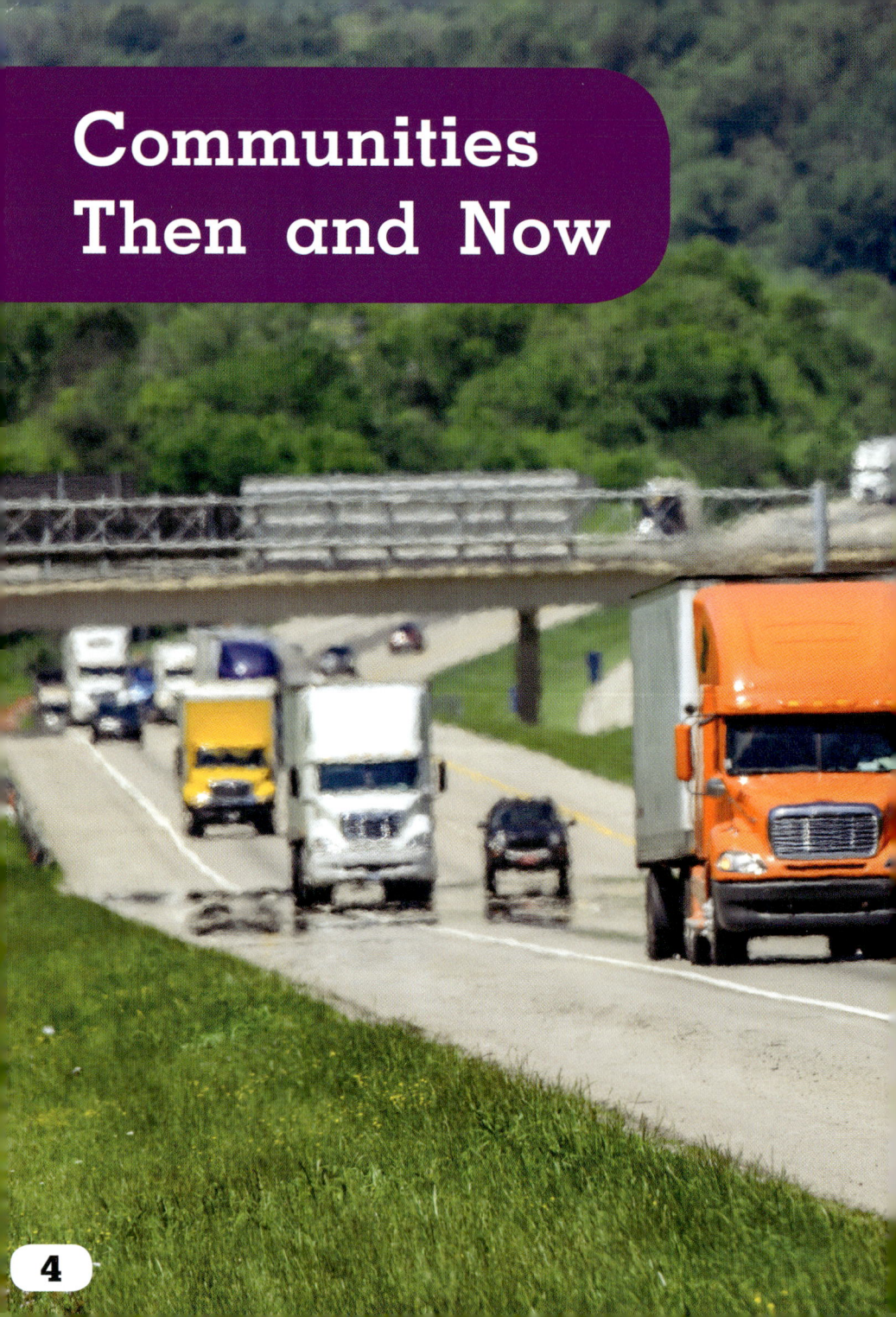
Communities Then and Now

Trees were here.
Now there is a road.

A factory was here.
Now there are homes.

A field was here.
Now it is an airport.

A train track was here. Now it is a bike path.

A farm was here.
Now it is a mall.

A small park was here.
Now it is a big park!

Did You See It?

airport

homes

mall

park

Index

airport, 9
bike path, 11
factory, 7
homes, 7

mall, 13
park, 15
road, 5
train track, 11